For Zoe ~ S S

For Clare ~ C P

LITTLE TIGER PRESS LTD,

1 Coda Studios, 189 Munster Road, London SW6 6AW

First published in Great Britain 2018

This edition published 2019

www.littletiger.co.uk

Text copyright © Suzy Senior 2018

Illustrations copyright © Claire Powell 2018

A CIP catalogue record for this book
is available from the British Library

Printed in China • LTP/1400/2282/0418

10 9 8 7 6 5 4 3 2 1

OCTOPANTS

Suzy Senior ◉ Claire Powell

LITTLE TIGER
LONDON

Hello there! I'm an octopus.
There's something you should know . . .

I don't have any underpants.
I've nothing on below!

I tried to buy some octopants.
I tried all over town.

Clam Closet

But everyone just laughed and laughed,
then answered with a frown . . .

BARGAIN ☆ BUCKET

"Underpants? For you?" they said.
"Oh, no. We don't have ANY.
The problem seems to be your legs –
you've just got six too many!"

I've even tried to shop online.
I tried to surf the net.
I found a cod, three tuna,
and my credit card got wet!

I still could NOT find octopants,
 it almost made me cry.
There's pants out there for everyone,
 except for octopi.

But then one day I found a place
I hadn't seen before.
A seahorse hovered just inside
the huge revolving door.

"Good morning! Can I help you, sir?
Why don't you step inside?
My Under-Sea Emporium
is famous ocean-wide."

"I have bobble hats
for barnacles . . .

and evening wear for eels . . .

Onesies just for urchins . . .

and slipper socks for seals."

"Jewellery for jellyfish . . .

water wings for whales . . .

And rainbow paint for rainbow trout
to smarten up their scales. "

"Yes! I've got clothes for EVERYONE,
with spots and stripes and rockets,
Pirate ships and sparkly bits,
and lots of handy pockets!"

"Now . . . underwear for you, sir?
I think you've been misled.
Perhaps you don't need octopants
but something else instead?"

And then I saw the problem.
I'd looked at this all wrong.
These legs weren't legs.
These legs were ARMS,
and had been, all along!

Hello there, I'm an octopus.
  By now, you might have guessed –
I'm STILL not wearing underpants . . .

CHANGING ROOM

MAXIMUM 8 LEGS

I bought an
OCTO-VEST!

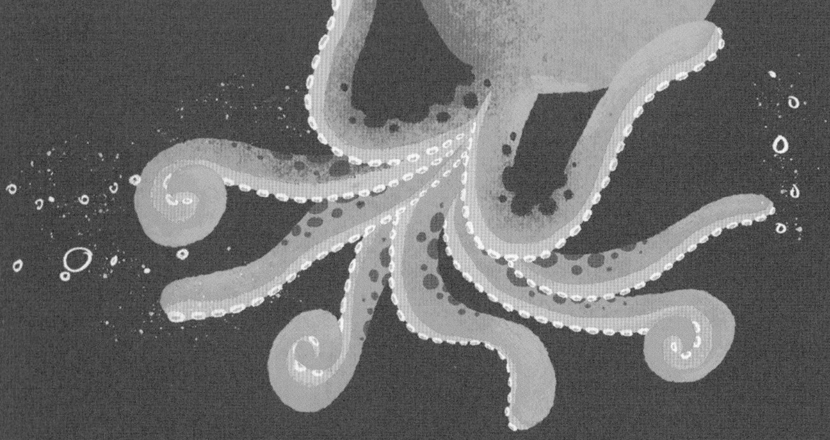

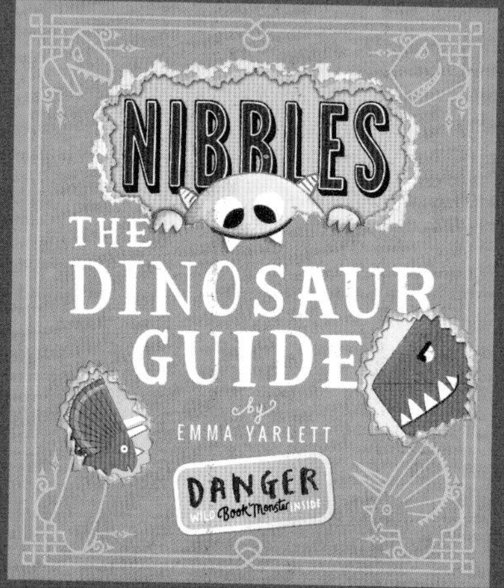

Find your perfect fit with these hilarious adventures from Little Tiger!

For information regarding any of the above titles or for our catalogue, please contact us: Little Tiger Press, 1 Coda Studios, 189 Munster Road, London SW6 6AW
Tel: 020 7385 6333 • E-mail: contact@littletiger.co.uk • www.littletiger.co.uk